World of Reading

P9-DDC-560

LEVEL 1
+ FUN ANIMAL FACTS

Disney Junior

PUPPY DOG PALS

Pups on a
MISSION

Adapted by LORI FROEB
Based on the series created by HARLAND WILLIAMS
Illustrated by the DISNEY STORYBOOK ART TEAM

First Paperback Edition, September 2018
1 3 5 7 9 10 8 6 4 2

ISBN 978-1-368-02044-2
FAC-029261-18181
Library of Congress Control Number: 2017963702
Manufactured in the United States of America
For more Disney Press fun, visit www.disneybooks.com

SUSTAINABLE
FORESTRY
INITIATIVE
Certified Sourcing
www.sfiprogram.org
SFI-01415

Disney PRESS
Los Angeles • New York

Bob is home!

Bingo and Rolly are happy to see him.

They bark. They wag their tails.

Bob says, "Let's play ball."

DOGS USE THEIR BARKS TO COMMUNICATE WITH HUMANS AND OTHER ANIMALS.

The puppies do not
know where their ball is.

Bob does not know where their ball is, either.

A DOG'S SENSE OF SMELL CAN BE A THOUSAND TIMES BETTER THAN A HUMAN'S.

Hissy thinks she saw the ball in
the kitchen.
The pups run to the kitchen.

The ball is not by the toaster.

The ball is not in the fridge.

The pups run to the living room.
The ball is not under the pillows.
The ball is not on the bookshelf.

The pups make a mess.
A.R.F. cleans up the mess.
The pups still cannot find the ball.

**PUGS ARE CURIOUS AND
TEND TO GET INTO MISCHIEF.**

The pups have a mission:
FIND THEIR BALL!
Bingo and Rolly collar up.

They run to the backyard.
They look in the sandbox.
The ball is not in the sandbox.

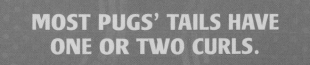

The gopher thinks he saw
the ball at the dog park.

Bingo and Rolly run to the dog park.

The pups look inside the tube slide.
They do not find the ball.
They find Cupcake.

Cupcake thinks she saw a
big dog with their ball.

Bingo and Rolly find the big dog.
She does not have their ball.

The big dog thinks the squirrel has their ball.

The pups find the squirrel.
He does not have their ball.

The squirrel thinks he saw
their ball at the farm.

**A SQUIRREL'S FRONT TEETH
NEVER STOP GROWING!**

Rolly and Bingo run to the farm.
The ball is not in the pigpen.

**PIGS ROLL IN THE
MUD TO KEEP COOL.**

The ball is not in the henhouse.

The puppies are sad.
Where can their ball be?

The pups see a bird.
The bird thinks he saw the ball
at the beach.

**BIRDS HAVE HOLLOW
BONES TO HELP THEM FLY.**

The pups run to the beach.
Bingo looks for the ball.
Rolly looks at a crab.

Rolly digs and digs.

Rolly digs some more.
Bingo spots a boat.

PUGS ARE KNOWN AS A TOY BREED,
BECAUSE THEY ARE SO SMALL.

"That boat looks like our bath toy," says Bingo.

"We play with bath toys in the bathtub," says Rolly.

"We play with our ball in the bathtub, too," Bingo says.

The pups run home.
They know just where to look.

Their ball is right where they left it.
It is in the tub!

Mission accomplished!
Time to play ball.